THE KITES ARE FLYING!

Books by the same author

Half a Man

Homecoming

I Believe in Unicorns

Meeting Cézanne

The Mozart Question

My Father Is a Polar Bear

This Morning I Met a Whale

Beowulf

Hansel and Gretel

The Pied Piper of Hamelin

Singing for Mrs Pettigrew

Sir Gawain and the Green Knight

THE KITES ARE FLYING!

Michael Morpurgo

illustrated by
Laura Carlin

WALKER BOOKS

First published 2009 by
Walker Books Ltd, 87 Vauxhall Walk, London SE11 5HJ

This edition published 2016

2 4 6 8 10 9 7 5 3

Text © 2009 Michael Morpurgo
Illustrations © 2009 Laura Carlin

This book has been typeset in Adobe Caslon

Printed and bound in Great Britain by Clays Ltd, St Ives plc

British Library Cataloguing in Publication Data:
a catalogue record for this book is available from the British Library

ISBN 978-1-4063-6731-7

www.walker.co.uk

*For the children who live on
both sides of the wall, who will
one day bring it tumbling down.
No guns or trumpets needed.*
M.M.

For Maia, Molly and Smudge
L.C.

1st May 2008

Nearly midnight. Gruesome hotel.
Jerusalem airport.

Wish I wasn't here.
Sometimes I really do
wonder why I write a
diary at all. It's useful
enough I suppose when
I'm actually filming –
helps me to remember
details I might forget,
the sequence of events,
and so on. But on nights
like this I know I'm

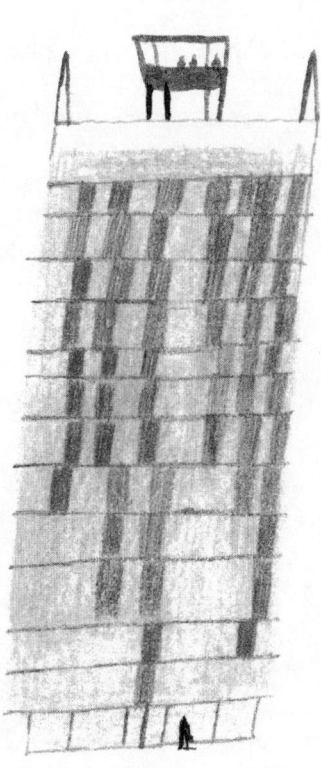

doing it just out of habit. I've written in my diary every day since I can remember. I can see the point of it after the truly memorable days, but then I would probably remember those anyway. The truth is that there have been so many days I just want to forget. Days like today.

Traffic jams all the way to the airport. Late arriving. Ages checking in. Plane delayed anyway, so I needn't have expended all that fury and frustration. Can't those security people at least try to smile while they're rifling through your bag? I mean, what's their problem? Then we had to fly into the most violent turbulence I've ever known. I should be used to it by now – I do enough flying. But this time I really did think my number was up. Some of the lockers flew open, and the lady next to me started saying her prayers. We didn't land at Jerusalem. We bumped. Bumpity, bumpity, bump. It was as if the pilot was reverting to his childhood. The plane was a stone he was skimming across a lake. On and on it went, and we were inside it. Then there were more unsmiling security people. Late into this ghastly airport hotel where I know I'm not going to sleep. The sheets and towels stink of chemicals. The only air I can breathe is noisy, because I can't switch off the air-conditioning.

When I phoned home for a bit of comfort, Penny said everything was fine. She sounded a bit sleepy, but she said I hadn't woken her up. Jamie had been a bit hyper apparently when he came home from school, but he was fast asleep now. She'd read him his King Arthur book, again. She told me that Jamie said I read it better than she did. She was a bit miffed about that. But I wasn't. It made me smile, probably my first smile all day. Makes a fellow feel better to smile. Penny told me she missed me, that she wished I could be at home, and then we wouldn't have to be phoning each other in the middle of the night. "Max, do you realize what time it is?" she said. She wasn't cross exactly, but I could tell she didn't want to talk much after that. I felt very alone after she put the phone down. Still do. Mustn't get gloomy. Got to sleep. Can't be gloomy if you're asleep. Early start tomorrow. Must find out about the buses first thing. The food on the plane was

disgusting. I only ate it because it was there, which was pretty stupid. And now I've got bellyache.

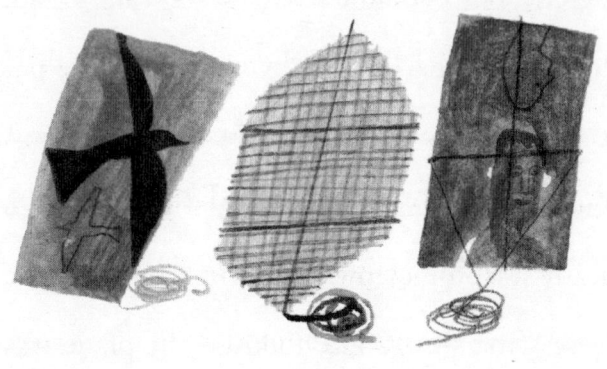

Hey, Mahmoud, are you there? Are you there? Can you hear me? I had my beautiful dream again last night, the same dream, about the kites. Uncle Yasser says it is a foolish dream. But it isn't foolish, is it, Mahmoud?

You're always telling me not to listen to old Uncle Gasbag. It's your dream, that's what you say. You dream what you want to dream, little brother. I like it when you call me little brother. You know something? You're not only my big brother, you're my best friend. Hey, I saw that girl again, the one in the blue headscarf. She was there again today, waving to me, and she was in my dream too. She was waving to me then as well. She does it every time!

Mahmoud, are you listening? I'm afraid to close my eyes in case I have that nightmare again. You told me the nightmares would go away when the dream comes true. What was it you said? "You only dream the beautiful dream, little brother, because of the nightmare. It's like day always follows night. You can't have the one without the other. Light is only light," you said, "when you've seen how dark the dark is." I still don't understand that, Mahmoud. There's a lot you tell me I don't really understand. But I don't mind. I like it when you talk to me. I like it so much. Will you fly my kite with me tomorrow? Will you be there under the kite tree?

It's the same every time I have to go to bed. I want to go on talking to you all night long, Mahmoud. I suppose I shouldn't talk to you as much as I do – you must get fed up with me – but there's no one else I can talk to, no one else I want to talk to, either; no one else who knows, no one else who was there. You are my big brother, 12 years old – that's four years

older than me – and I tell you everything. I'm always thinking about you, even when I'm not talking to you. I'm so proud of you – the fastest runner in the whole village! But you're more than just my big brother, you've been the father of the family, too, since Father was taken away by the occupiers and put in a prison camp back when I was little. We haven't seen him since. So you have had to help out on the farm with Uncle Yasser, Uncle Gasbag.

Everything you have ever planted grows well – Uncle Yasser says it's your green fingers. Broad beans, aubergines, sunflowers, olives, lemons – they all grow. But you have always liked the sheep best of all, sitting on the hillside all day long looking after the sheep. You know all of them, and they know you. They love you and they trust you. It's like you're their big brother too. I like being out there with you and the sheep, Mahmoud. I like feeling

the warm wind on my face, and smelling the wild thyme. We lie there watching the hawks hovering on the wind. We talk, we laugh, we dream. You are a dreamer too, like me. I think we even dream the same dreams.

But we don't lie out there on the hillside just dreaming. We make our kites, and we fly them. When I hold the spool and let out the string, you race out over the hillside, whooping and yelling as the kite catches the wind. Then it's up there, and flying high.

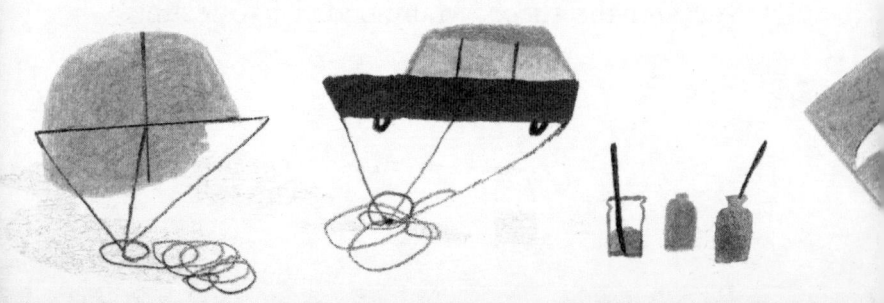

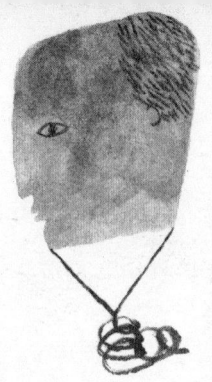

You make the kite swoop and soar, again and again. Sometimes it crashes into a tree, or dives into the hillside. You are always angry with yourself then, and won't speak to me. But after a while, when you've calmed down, I tell you that maybe we should just mend it, or make another one, and we do. Each one we make is better than before – different, bigger, smaller, with a longer tail, maybe, or a shorter one. They're all painted different colours, too – some like birds, some like butterflies, some

even like fish. On summer evenings the whole village comes out to watch us. They stand there, gazing up into the sky and loving our kites as much as we do. It's the only time we can forget all our troubles and sadnesses and just be happy again, for a while, anyway.

You remember that afternoon, Mahmoud, when I asked you why kites seem to make everyone so happy, why people laugh out loud when they see them soaring up there in the sky. I remember every word you told me, Mahmoud, as if it was yesterday. But it wasn't yesterday, it was two years ago next week.

"Every time I fly a kite, little brother, I'm thinking it's me up there, and that I'm far away from all this down here, far away from the soldiers and the checkpoints and the tanks. Up there I'm out of it. I go wherever the wind takes me, and no one can stop me. No soldiers, no checkpoints, no tanks," you said.

And then you were angry, Mahmoud. Whenever you talked about the occupiers you always got angry. And that time you cried. You cried because you were so angry. "Why do they keep Father in prison, Said?" you asked me. "Tell me that. Why do they come here and take our lands? Why do they treat us like donkey muck? Why can't they just go home and leave us in peace?" Then you told me about the soldier. "I want to tell you something,

Said," you said. "It happened yesterday. I can't stop thinking about it. I saw this soldier. He was down at the checkpoint, and I was coming across the road driving the sheep. He was looking straight down the barrel of his rifle into my eyes. Then I saw his face under the helmet. I couldn't believe it, he didn't look any older than me. I'm thinking, you're someone's son too. I'm thinking, one day you're going to kill me, maybe, and you won't

even know why you're doing it. Do you know
what I did then? I smiled at him. I didn't want
to look frightened, so I smiled at him, just to
show him. He smiled back, I promise you he
did, even gave me a wink.

So then I'm thinking
that they can't be all bad,
these occupiers. There's
the girl in the blue
headscarf who waves to

me over the wall sometimes, and this soldier. That's two. So if they're not all bad, and we're not all bad, why can't the good ones on both sides just get together and sort it all out? Then the soldiers could all go home, and Father could be let out of prison and come home to us, and everything would be right again." There were tears running down your cheeks and I remember you brushed them away with the back of your hand. "I miss Father, Said," you said. "Sometimes I miss him so much that it hurts."

You know the honest truth, Mahmoud? I hardly remember Father. He's been gone so long. I know him mostly from those photos

Mother shows me. But I don't like looking at them because Mother always cries when she talks about him, and I hate it. When she cries it's like my whole head is filling up with tears, like it's bursting with sadness. I like it much better when you tell me about Father, because you've told me so many funny stories about him. I love it when I'm sitting under the kite tree and thinking about the things you told me about him, how Father taught you everything you know: how to make kites, how to plant broad beans, how to whistle the sheep in, how to play football. I remember I told you once you were rubbish at football, and you wrestled me onto my back and sat on top of me, threatening to tickle me to death unless I took it back. So I took it back. "Anyway, little brother, do you think anyone at Barcelona or Manchester United makes better kites than me?" That's what you said. Then you tickled me half to death, and we rolled over and over, screeching and giggling. We looked up and there were all the sheep staring at us as if we were completely mad, which made us laugh all the more. We laugh a lot, don't we, Mahmoud? I love to hear you laugh.

Mahmoud? Are you there? I was thinking about you again this afternoon, under the kite tree. It's a good place for thinking. But I talk to you best when I'm in bed at night, don't I?

I don't know why. Maybe it's because it's more secret. But the kite tree's my favourite place in the whole world. I love that old tree. Uncle Gasbag says it's the oldest tree on the hillside, at least ten grandfathers old. That's why it's all twisted and crooked, just like he is. It's the best shade on the whole farm, so the sheep love it too. We've put a lot of kites together under that tree, haven't we? It's our kite tree, yours and mine, Mahmoud. That's why it's the place I most love to be – because you're always there. And that's where I was this afternoon when I first saw him.

I could see someone walking along the road down in the valley. He'd just got off the bus. I knew right away he wasn't one of us. None of us would wear a hat like that. And I knew he wasn't an occupier from the settlement on the other side of the wall. They don't wear hats like that either. He kept stopping every now and again to look around him, as if it was all new to him, as if he was a stranger.

Then he saw me, saw the sheep and the kite tree. He turned off the road and began climbing up the hillside towards me. He had a rucksack on his back, and that silly hat on his head, and he had some kind of equipment slung over his shoulder. And I'm thinking, he's one of those television reporters, that's what he is. We see them coming through the village often enough, don't we? But usually they're in Land Rovers, and usually there's lots of them. But this one was alone, and on foot. And I thought, I don't want him to come any closer. He's going to disturb the sheep, I know he is. They're already getting up and moving away. They don't like strangers any more than I do. Best to stay where I am and ignore him. I'll get on with my kite and hope he'll just go away. But then I thought that maybe, before he goes away, I might get some chocolate off him. Television people are always fair game for chocolate, and sometimes dollars, too,

if you're lucky. I know how it works: if you want to get lucky with these reporter guys then you have to smile at them, and do it as if you mean it. You have to call them "Mister", too – you told me that, Mahmoud, remember? I can't call him "Mister" but I can look up at him and smile.

When I did, I saw he was just a few steps away from me, taking off his silly hat and wiping his brow with the back of his hand. He was all puffed out from the climb. He took off his rucksack and put all his equipment down on the ground right beside me.

I'm telling you, Mahmoud. He's got the coolest camera I've ever seen in all my life!

I didn't want chocolates any more. I didn't even want dollars. I just wanted to hold that camera. I wanted to make a movie with it. I love movies. You love movies too, don't you. *ET, Shrek*. I liked *Shrek 2* best. The donkey – I love that donkey.

Are you there, Mahmoud? Are you there?

2nd May

*Roof of village house
(don't yet know the name
of the village, will find out
tomorrow) West Bank. 11.10 p.m.*

Now I know why I make films. I need reminding sometimes, and today has reminded me. It's to capture moments, great moments, so that they are held for ever on film, so that one fleeting day does not simply merge into the next fleeting day and become part of the blur of existence. I feel tonight as if I'm really living inside a story, that I'm a part of it. I'm no longer merely reporting on it. I'm not sure this has ever happened to me quite like this before.

I have the night sky starry above me, and I'm writing by torchlight. These are the same stars that were shining over 2,000 years ago, on the first Christmas night. That was the picture of this land that I grew up with as a child – it was a place of shepherds and angels and stables and stars. Of course I've learnt since that the Holy Land wasn't at peace then, and it most certainly isn't now. The images are all too familiar: the bombed-out buses, the tanks and soldiers in the streets, the stone-throwing children, the masked gunmen marching, the hilltop settlements, the squalor of the refugee camps, the funerals, the burials, the grief.

But I'm here for the wall. It's the wall more than anything that has haunted me. It's the wall that has brought me here.

It all depends on how old you are. For some people it is the television footage of the assassination of President Kennedy, or the pictures of Neil Armstrong stepping down onto the surface of the moon. For others it might be Nelson Mandela walking out of prison in South Africa, or it might be those planes slamming into the Twin Towers of Manhattan. For most of us there is a happening we have witnessed at an impressionable time of our lives that we shall never forget. For me as a youngster, it was sitting on the floor with a bunch of college friends watching in utter astonishment as the Berlin Wall came tumbling down in front of our eyes. It was the day when people decided enough was enough, and they wanted to be free. They climbed up onto the wall and began to pull it down with their bare hands, this wall that had divided the world for so long and had brought us to the brink of nuclear war. To see that wall coming down was the single most hopeful, most momentous time of my young life. I wrote about it in my diary, copiously, pages and pages of it, rambling stuff when I read it now, romantic, rapturously optimistic. But I was young then.

Now another wall has been built – nothing new about walls, of course, Hadrian's Wall, the Great Wall of China, and plenty of others. But this one is now, and, like the Berlin Wall, the passions it arouses threaten once more to engulf the world in global conflict. I had to come to see it for myself. I want to make a film, tell the story, but from both sides of the wall, Palestinian, then Israeli. I want to find out how it is to live in the shadow of this wall, to tell a story that does not point the finger,

that does not accuse, but tells it as it is. That was my plan, and it still is. But today, the first day of filming, hasn't worked out at all as I'd imagined it would. The totally unexpected has happened.

I've discovered over the years that if you travel by bus or train, you get close to people, get to talk to them if you're lucky. Cars isolate you. So I've been travelling on buses for most of the day. Lots of dust, lots of checkpoints, some filming as I went, but not too much –

I didn't want to attract attention. I did the last leg of my journey up to this village on foot, and that was when I came across the shepherd boy.

It was late afternoon. He was sitting alone on the hillside under an ancient olive tree with a gnarled and spiralling trunk. He had his sheep all around him. Until that moment I had seen nothing even remotely picturesque in this tragic land, little that reminded me in any way of its Biblical past. All I'd seen were newly built hilltop settlements, green valleys below, and scattered across the landscape as far as the eye could see, small, straggling stone-built villages. And everywhere there was the wall, snaking its way around the hills, a symbol of oppression and occupation for one side, a protective defensive partition for the other.

The shepherd boy at once made me forget all that. He was making a kite, and was clearly so intent upon it that he did not even notice me coming. He was whistling softly as I came climbing up the hill towards him, not so much to make a tune, I thought, as to reassure his sheep. When he did look up at me, he showed no surprise or alarm. He looked about the same age as Jamie, perhaps a little older, and had the same sort of smile, too, open-hearted and engaging. I felt I couldn't wander on past him with just a wave or a meaningless nod of the head. And anyway, I needed a rest after

my long and exhausting
trudge up the hill. So I
stopped, sat down under
the tree and offered him
a drink out of my ruck-

sack. He shook his head at first, but when
I pressed him he took the bottle and drank
eagerly. When he handed the bottle back, he
said nothing. He wasn't talkative but he wasn't
sullen either. When I told him my name, he
didn't seem to want to tell me his. I could
see then that he wasn't a bit interested in me
anyway. It was my video camera. He couldn't
take his eyes off my video camera. It's a new
one, the latest Sony; digital, state-of-the-art

technology, light, neat, beautifully designed and made; the best I've ever worked with. The shepherd boy seemed in awe of it; completely fascinated. I thought that maybe this was the way we might make some kind of contact, a way to get talking, through my video camera. It seemed like a good idea.

When I offered to let him hold it, his whole face lit up. But I could tell pretty soon that just holding it wasn't going to be enough. So I showed him all the functions, how to work everything. He never spoke a word, but I knew he was taking everything in. Soon he was making it quite clear that he wanted to have a go with it. Having gone this far, I could hardly refuse. We walked out from under the tree, looking for something to film. Almost at once he was pointing up into the sky. There was a hawk hovering there, so I let him film it. Afterwards he wanted to film the sheep, then me in my hat. He liked my hat a lot, I could tell that. But he did not even try to speak to me, and I thought that was strange. We sat

down under the tree again, and watched the replay of his film. He insisted on seeing it over and over again.

I wanted to get him to talk, so I tried to explain to him as best I could that this was what I did, that I was a cameraman and that I had come to make a film about the wall. It was obvious he didn't understand a word I was saying. I kept on trying. But whether I spoke in English or in the few words of Arabic I know, it made no difference. His smile was the only response I got. He just didn't seem to want to talk, yet I had the distinct impression that he wanted me to go on talking. And I certainly got the feeling that he was quite happy for me to stay. Or maybe it was just that he wanted my camera to stay. He still could hardly keep his eyes off it.

I could see that talking wasn't getting me anywhere. So I decided I would get on and do what I had come here for. I got to my feet, picked up the camera and indicated that I wanted to film him – him and his sheep. "Do you mind?" I asked him. "Is it all right?" Still he wouldn't speak. He just smiled and shrugged, and I wasn't sure whether this meant yes or no. I didn't want to risk upsetting him, so I sat down again and we lapsed into silence, the sheep gathering all around us again under the shade of the olive tree, their smell pungent and heavy in the warm air. When the shepherd boy began to work on his kite again, I thought maybe I had outstayed my welcome. But then, quite suddenly, he reached across, picked up my camera and handed it to me. Permission granted! I knew then that this boy must understand a whole lot more than his silence lets on.

I began with a wide-angle shot of the shepherd boy under the tree, with the kite on his lap, his sheep all around him and the wall in the distance. None of it was any use, though, because he would keep looking up at the camera and smiling, and holding up his half-made kite to show me. He put my hat on his head and began to mimic me filming him. He was good, too. I recognized my body language instantly. But it was pointless to go on filming. We shared what food we had. He took a great fancy to my chocolate digestive biscuits – Jamie's going-away present to me – and he gave me some pinenuts out of his pocket. We shared our silence, too. It was the best we could manage, and maybe after all, I thought,

 as good a way as any to get to know one another. I showed him the photo I keep in my wallet of Penny and Jamie and me in the garden at home in London. He liked

that. He looked at it intently for a very long time before he gave it back. Then, with evening coming on, he stood up and began to whistle his sheep home. I thought it was time for me to set off on my way too.

I followed him, the sheep clambering around me, bleating at me. It was a steep climb, and very soon I was finding it hard to keep up. Ahead of me the boy was springing from rock to rock, as agile as his sheep. I thought I could do the same. Vanity, vanity. Where he could leap, I could leap. No problem. Wrong.

I landed awkwardly, felt my ankle twist under me and found myself sitting there in amongst the rocks clutching my ankle, moaning and cursing all at the same time. The shepherd boy came running back. He got me to my feet and put his arm around me to support me. I hobbled with him all the way up into the village. His arm was strong around me, stronger than I'd have thought possible for a boy of his size.

Half an hour or so later I found myself sitting in the boy's home, my ankle throbbing less now in a bowl of cold water, surrounded by his large extended family all talking to each other – about me I was sure – and watching me, if not with open hostility, then certainly with some suspicion. They were polite but wary. The boy, I noticed, still did not speak, even amongst his own family. He was proudly showing them the progress he'd made on his kite that day. I could see he was a much treasured child.

We ate lamb, and the most succulent broad beans I've ever tasted, and sweetly spiced cake dripping with honey. Luckily, there were still enough of my chocolate digestive biscuits to share around, so I could make some contribution, at least, to the feast. When the boy came and sat himself down beside me, I sensed he was doing so because

he wanted to make it very clear to everyone, including me, that I was his special guest. I felt honoured by that, and moved by his affection. But soon enough it dawned on me that he had another reason for sitting himself down next to me. He began tapping my arm and pointing at my camera. He wanted to hold it again, to demonstrate to his family that he knew precisely how it worked. He still didn't speak, not a word. He just showed them. He put on my hat, and made believe he was me. He was the cameraman, turning the camera on each of them, and last of all on me, too. Then he was going into a whole performance, acting out how I'd fallen over in the rocks. There I was clutching my ankle and rolling about in agony, rocking back and forth, then hobbling back home, leaning on him. He had everyone in fits by now – me, too. Later he came fishing in my pocket for my wallet. He found the photo and passed it around so that everyone in the family could have a good look. It was this, as much as all his showing off and playacting, that broke down some of their reserve towards me. I think the

boy knew they would look at me differently once they'd seen the photo. That's why he did it, I'm sure.

The boy used almost exactly the same method of postponing bedtime as Jamie. His delaying tactics are only different in one respect: he goes about it entirely silently. Jamie's protests are infinitely noisier. But they share the same absolute determination not to go to bed. The boy was appealing directly to his mother, yet at the same time pleading his case to everyone, that he needed more time to finish his kite. He did this skilfully, wordlessly, making it quite clear to all of us what it was that still needed to be done, and that it was really unfair to expect him to go to bed until it was finished. All he needed was just a little more time to finish it. The mistake he made was that in the end he did finish it. He was still protesting as his mother hustled him off to bed, leaving me alone with his family.

Once he'd gone there followed a long and awkward silence. After a time I decided it was up to me to try to end it. I thought the best way of doing this might be to venture a word or two in Arabic.

"A fine boy," I said – that's what I thought I'd said, anyway; that's what I hoped I'd said. There were smiles all around. I must have said the right thing, in more or less the right way. But the silver-bearded man on my left was still suspicious of me. I took him to be the head of the family. He certainly looked the oldest, and he seemed to be the one to whom everyone else deferred. When he spoke to me it was in quite good English, and with very little hesitation.

"I am Yasser Hussein. I am Said's uncle. I wish to say that you are welcome in our home. You have been kind to Said, and for this we are grateful. As you say, he is a fine boy, but he is a troubled boy."

"He is very quiet," I said. "He does not say very much. My son Jamie, back at home, he's the noisy kind." The old man translated what I'd said for the others. The whole room seemed suddenly filled with sadness. He turned back to me, looking me full in the eye now. It was a searching gaze, and very disconcerting, but I returned it as best I could. It was an uncomfortably long while before he spoke again.

"You are a television reporter?"

"Yes."

"Whose side are you on? Theirs or ours?"

"I'm on no one's side." Still that same penetrating look.

"But you are Said's true friend?"

"Yes."

"Then maybe there is something you should know. Said cannot tell you this himself, because he cannot speak. Not any more. There was a time, not so long ago, when he was, as you say your son is, noisy; very noisy. And like

Mahmoud, Said speaks good English, better than me. They learn it at school, but more from films on the television, I think. I tell you, you could not stop Said from talking."

"I don't understand," I said.

"None of us understand," he told me. "None of us will ever understand. All we know is that it was God's will. And it must be God's will also that you come here to our house. It is good you come here, because you make Said smile and laugh. Your camera makes him smile. Your hat makes him laugh. We like to see this. It is good for him to be happy again. We hope always for the best for Said, we pray for it. We are all very proud of him.

Maybe he does not speak, but he is the best shepherd boy in all of Palestine. He knows all of the sheep by name, every one of them, just like Mahmoud. And like Mahmoud he makes the best kites in all of Palestine. But Said's kites are not ordinary kites, you know, not like anyone else's kites."

"What do you mean?" I asked him.

"Maybe he will show you that himself," he told me. "Maybe he will fly his kite for you tomorrow. This one is almost ready to fly, I think. But for Said the wind must be perfect.

The wind must be always from the east, and not too strong, or Said will not fly his kites."

He got up then, and when he did, everyone did. He was still unsmiling as he said goodnight. I felt I had passed a kind of test, but an important one. The evening was over.

My ankle still feels a bit tender. It's swollen, too, but I don't think it's as bad as I thought. I can wriggle my toes. Hurt like hell when it happened, but nothing is broken. Just a sprain. I can't put much weight on it. They've given me a stick. I can manage, just about. I have to. There's no way I'm going to miss going out with Said and his sheep tomorrow. I just hope the wind is right, and that he does fly his kite.

That's something I have to be there to film. I know now that it isn't just me that Said doesn't speak to. He can't speak at all. Or he won't. I want to know why. Why can't he speak? And who is this Mahmoud that Said's Uncle Yasser was on about? There are so many things I've got to find out about. Tomorrow. Tomorrow.

Hey, Mahmoud. Are you listening? Are you there? It's dark. I don't want to sleep. I want to talk to you.

This man, Mahmoud, he's not like any of the television reporters who've been to the village before. I will tell you about this man, Mahmoud. All right, so he's a bit clumsy on his feet, but his chocolate biscuits must be the best in the whole world. And he's kind, too. He let us have all of them, enough for everyone in the family, and he didn't even have one himself. That's not all. I mean, you have to check out his video camera! Smartest camera you've ever seen. Sony, digital, and he let me use it! I got to hold it myself, and he showed me how to work it. And, and, and … he let me make a real film, all on my own. Sort of on my own, anyway. The hawk came flying over the kite tree, hovering there just like he does every evening, and Mister Max taught me how to hold the camera tight and steady, how to zoom in on him close and hold the shot. You know something, Mahmoud? When I

was looking through the lens I was so close to that hawk that I could see every one of his wing feathers trembling in the wind. I'm not kidding. It was like he was near enough for me just to reach out and touch him. And Mister Max has got a son back home. He looks a bit like you, Mahmoud. Got a big nose, and lots of teeth when he smiles. I've seen a photo.

Anyway, Mister Max went and tripped over, which was very funny, but he's done his ankle in, which is why he's been sitting down there with his foot in that bowl of water. Like I told you, he's a bit clumsy. I brought him home. I had to. Couldn't leave him there, could I? You should've seen Uncle Gasbag's face when he saw us. You know what he's like, hates all reporters, says he doesn't trust them. What am I doing bringing one of his kind into our home? Don't I know they're all liars, all on the side of the occupiers? But Mother likes Mister Max because he likes her honey cake, and the others all like him too on account of the film he let me make ... and because of the chocolate biscuits. Even Uncle Yasser liked the camera. You know what I think? I think that sometimes Uncle Gasbag just pretends to be a grumpy old goat. He's fixing up a crutch for Mister Max for tomorrow, so I think he liked him really.

Hey, Mahmoud. You should have seen

Mister Max eating his honey cake. He licked his fingers afterwards, just like you. Only without the loud slurping noise that always makes me laugh. So I laughed at Mister Max too, and then everyone laughed, even Uncle Yasser. Mahmoud, I think this has been the happiest day for a long time, since you … since it happened. Mahmoud? Are you still there, Mahmoud?

I want to tell you about something else. It's the kite I'm making. I'm having trouble with it. It's the glue again. The paper keeps coming away from the frame. I've mixed the glue properly, just like you taught me. All right, I might have hurried it a bit. I can hear you telling me, "Don't hurry it, Said. You always hurry things. Take your time. A kite will fly when it's ready to fly, in its own good time. It's like a living thing. It's not just paper and wood and string." I want to fly it tomorrow, Mahmoud. It's important. I want to show Mister Max how beautiful it is. I want the wind to be right. I want the girl in the blue headscarf to be there too. I won't fly it unless she's there. I never do. And I won't forget to wave to her for you, I promise.

I won't sleep. I know I won't. I've got too many thoughts whirling round and round in my head. I don't mind. I don't want to sleep anyway. I don't want to live through the nightmare. If I stay awake I won't have the nightmare. I'll stay awake. I'll talk to myself. That'll do it.

Everyone in the family thinks that flying the kites is a waste of time – except you, of course. But it isn't. And in the village they all know what I'm doing, and why I'm doing it, too. They shake their heads at me; they feel sorry for me. At school, they just think I'm mad. They don't say so, not out loud. But that's because of you, Mahmoud,

because they don't want to be unkind to your little brother. I see it in their eyes, though. Sometimes it really gets me down. I know, you've told me before, you're always telling me, I've got to keep going because it's the right dream to have, the right thing to do, the only way to work things out.

But there are some things you won't tell me, however much I ask. I want you to tell me why it had to happen like it did, why it had to be you, why the kite had to crash-land down in the valley that morning. Uncle Gasbag always says it was God's will. Oh, and that's supposed to make it all right, is it, Uncle? It wasn't God who was flying the kite, was it?

It was me. I was the one who crashed it. I was the one who was moaning on and on about how it wasn't fair that you flew the kites more than I did, how I only got to hold the spool and let out the string. If you hadn't given in to me like you did, if you hadn't let me fly the kite, none of it would have happened. If you'd been flying the kite yourself, you'd have controlled it better, kept it flying, I know you would. You wouldn't have panicked like I did, and the kite wouldn't have crashed down by the road. It probably wouldn't have crashed at all. You know how to fly kites better than anyone else in the whole village, in the whole world, Mahmoud, everyone knows that. You should have been flying it, not me. Then it wouldn't have happened, and you wouldn't have had to go running down the hill to pick it up. And if you hadn't gone there…

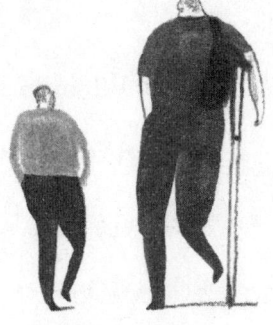

3rd May
10.30 p.m. Addulah Village.
Same rooftop. Another starry,
starry night.

Ankle's a lot better, thanks to the crutch. Wouldn't have been able to manage at all today without that. Still don't know which of them arranged it for me. It appeared from nowhere. I just found it beside me when I woke up. They're kind, these people, wonderfully kind. Long day. Good day. Important day. But it's been a sad day, too. I'm tired. Hobbling about like Long John Silver all day has been exhausting, but I think maybe I might be making the most extraordinary film I've ever made. Difficult to remember everything that's happened, but I'll try. It's been a day I never want to forget.

I was up before dawn and went, alone, down into the valley. I needed to film the sun coming up over the wall. I wanted to capture a whole day in this place, sunrise to sunset. After I'd filmed the dawn, I climbed back up the hill so that I could get a long shot of the wall from just below the village – I had to have

the villagers' constant view of it. I tracked it up through the olive groves and over the hillside to the settlement beyond where the flag flies. The more I look at it, the more I want to see the wall from their side, too. Do they feel just as imprisoned by the wall over there as these people do? I have to find out. Dogs barked at one another from both sides, cocks crowed, donkeys brayed.

After breakfast I went off with Said and his sheep, Said carrying some of my equipment as well as his kite, now with string and spool attached. That was when I first saw there was some writing in Arabic on one side of the kite, but I didn't know what it meant, and I couldn't ask him. I doubted he'd be flying his kite that day anyway, because there wasn't a breath of wind.

A couple of hours later, though, as I was sitting under the kite tree with the sheep browsing in amongst the rocks, I felt a sudden wind spring up. Said was on his feet at once. He ran out onto the open hillside and stood there for a while, his head lifted into the wind. I was filming him surreptitiously from under the tree. I think he knew I was, but by now he was paying no attention at all to me, nor to the camera. Clearly he had something much more important on his mind. Then I saw him turn and wave at me, frantically. He came

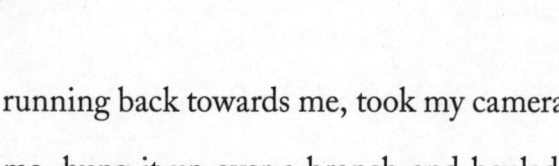

running back towards me, took my camera off me, hung it up over a branch and hauled me to my feet.

He thrust the spool into my hands, showed me what to do and went racing out over the hill with the kite. I watched him holding it high, letting it go, saw the wind take it and fly it. I marvelled at the beauty of it, wondered at the exhilaration on his face. But it was only when he took the spool from me, handed me the string and let me fly it, that I felt that same joy for myself. The kite was wind-whipped and soaring above us, tugging to be free, longing to go higher, and Said was jumping up and down in wild delight as it swooped and hovered overhead. It was an old joy I had almost forgotten. I had done it like this with my father when I was a boy – I had tried it with Jamie a few times, but there was never enough wind, or maybe we just weren't very good at it. This was supreme. The kite was alive at the end of the string, loving it as much as I was. But all too soon, Said was tugging at my arm. He wanted the string back. I was just getting the hang of it and wasn't at all happy about giving it up, but I had no choice.

Said was a real expert. With a tweak of his wrist the kite turned and twirled. With a flick of his fingers he dived it and danced it. It was mesmerizing. But after a while I remembered

what I was there for, and my professional instinct kicked in. I had to have boy and kite in the same shot, so I needed to put some distance between them and me. I picked up my camera and began to film. I did not want to miss such an idyllic image. I closed on the fluttering kite, tracked its flight until the wall was there in the background. I tightened on the wall and tracked it up over the hillside, then zoomed in on the settlement beyond, on the blue and white flag flying there.

That was when I noticed there were some children in the street below, kicking a football about. When one of them scored, I could see there were the usual recriminations on one team and all the over-the-top celebrations on the other. Same the world over, I thought. When I turned my camera on Said again, I saw there was a frown of intense concentration on his face. I don't know how, but I think I knew what he was about to do, so when it happened it didn't really surprise me. He just let the kite go. It was quite deliberate. He simply gave it to the wind, holding his arms up as if he was releasing a trapped bird and giving it its freedom. The kite soared up high, floating there on the thermals before the wind discovered it and took it away over the olive grove, over the wall and up towards the hilltop settlement beyond.

I felt Said tugging insistently at my sleeve. He was trying to get the camera off me. He wasn't just wanting to have another go at filming, there was an urgency in his eyes. So I gave him the camera. He was looking through the lens across at the settlement. I saw at once what he was focussing on. There was a girl in a wheelchair. She was gazing up at the kite as it came floating down. When it landed, she wheeled herself over and picked it up. She was wearing a blue headscarf. For a few moments she sat there looking across at us, the kite on her lap, shielding her eyes against the sun as the footballers came racing over towards her. They stood there then, all of them gazing across the wall at us. Said handed me back the camera, and then he was waving both his hands in the air. Only the girl waved back, flourishing the kite above her head. The footballers were all drifting away by now. The two went on waving to one another for several minutes, long enough for me to film it. They didn't seem to want to stop.

On the way back home to the village that evening with the sheep we came across Uncle Yasser harvesting his broad beans. I stopped and asked if he'd mind if I filmed him at his work. He shrugged. "There is not much to film," he told me. "It's a poor crop, but it's always a poor crop. There's never enough water, that's the trouble. They have taken most of it. And they have taken all our best land for themselves. They leave us only the dust to farm in. So what can you do?" He was watching Said as he walked on up into the village with his sheep. "I see he has sent his kite away. He let it go. The wind must have been just right. He never keeps his kites, not one of them. He just makes another one, waits for the next east wind, and then sends it off again. Did you see what he writes on his kites? *Salaam*. This means 'peace'. And on every one of them he writes both their names,

Mahmoud and Said." I had not expected him to want to talk so willingly.

"How many has he sent?" I asked him.

"We are not sure. And he cannot tell us, of course. Maybe about one a week since Mahmoud ... and that was nearly two years ago now."

I felt I could ask, because I felt he wanted to tell me. "Who is this Mahmoud? What happened?" He gave me a long and hard look. I thought I had gone too far then, intruded too much. I stopped filming; I thought that was what he wanted.

"No," he said gravely. "You must film this. I want the world to hear about Mahmoud, about how he lived and how he died. You are Said's friend. I think he trusts you. I think he would want you to know. Only Said knows what happened. He was there. He saw it with his own eyes." I was filming him again now.

"Mahmoud was Said's older brother. He loved to make kites. He loved to fly kites, and always with Said. It happened two years ago next week, next Monday – before the occupiers built the wall. I knew there would be trouble that day, we all did. A settler's car was ambushed that morning, further down the valley. We heard that a woman was killed and her daughter was in hospital with bad injuries to her legs, that maybe she would die too. So we said to all the children in the village: this is a dangerous time, you must stay inside, everyone is safer inside if the soldiers come. But Mahmoud, like his father, was a strong-willed boy, and he became angry with me when I said he could not go out with the sheep and fly his kite. He told me the sheep had to go out, that he would fly his kite whenever and wherever he wanted, that they had put his father in prison, that he would

not let them make a prisoner of him in his own home, that he would not hide away like a coward. These were the last words Mahmoud spoke to me.

"And so they went off, the two of them together, with the sheep. Whenever Mahmoud went out, Said would always want to go with him. His mother tried to stop them, too. They wouldn't listen.

"Maybe an hour later, we heard a helicopter come flying low over the village. There was some shooting. When it was over we all ran outside. We saw Mahmoud lying at the bottom of the hill, beside the road. Said was with him, Mahmoud's head on his lap. When we got there, his eyes were open but he was dead. We asked Said how it happened. But he cannot tell us. Since that moment, he has not spoken. God willing, one day he will. God willing." His voice was breaking. He looked away from me, trying to compose himself. I was doing much the same thing. I couldn't bring myself to ask him any more questions. But when he turned to me again, I could see he was ready to tell me more.

"Said sent off his first kite the next day, the day we buried Mahmoud. Do you know why he sends his kites over there? He cannot tell us himself, of course, but we think that for Said every kite that lands over there in the settlement is like a seed of friendship. This is why he writes *salaam* on each one. We think that he hopes and believes that one day they'll send the kites back and everything will be right, that his father will come home from prison, that somehow friendships will grow, all the killing will stop, and peace will come. For Said, his kites are kites of peace. You know what I think? I think, let Said have his dreams. It's all he has. He'll find out soon enough what they're like over there. Many people tell him this. Uncle Gasbag I may be, but I know when a thing must not be spoken. Let him dream, I say, let him dream."

"But what about the girl?" I asked him. "The one with the blue headscarf, the one in the wheelchair. She picked up Said's kite. She waved at him. I saw her. She was trying to be friendly. It's a beginning, surely."

He wasn't having any of it. "I have seen this girl. We all have," he said. "She's alive, isn't she? It is Mahmoud who is dead, is it not? Tell me, what does it cost to wave? They cannot wave away what they did. She is an occupier, isn't she? They are all occupiers. All occupiers are the same."

I spent the evening here in the family house, on my knees on the floor with Said, helping him make his new kite, everyone

looking on. He caught my eye from time to time. I think there is so much he wants to tell me that he cannot. I see in his eyes someone who believes completely in his dream, and I know he wants me to believe in it too. I want to, but I'm finding that very hard. I think he can sense my doubt. I hope he can't.

I should have phoned home today, and now it's too late. Anyway, I'm too sad to talk, and it would be too difficult to explain how things are here over the phone. Tomorrow; I'll talk to them tomorrow.

One thing I've decided I have to do. When I film the wall from the other side, that has to be the settlement I go to. I have to go to where Said's sending his kites. I'm going to try to meet up with that girl in the wheelchair, to talk to those kids playing football. I have to see and hear the whole story, to know it as it's lived on both sides. Everything's as silent as the stars up here, and as beautiful as peace. Time to sleep. G'night, Jamie. G'night, Penny.

Hey, Mahmoud? Are you there, Mahmoud? Are you listening? I waved to the girl, Mahmoud, and she waved back too. That's 94 of our kites she's got now. Mahmoud? Mahmoud? You will stay with me, won't you? I don't want to go to sleep. I don't want the nightmare again. I want to stay awake and talk to you. Don't leave me.

You know how I hate the dark. I've got so much to tell you.

I flew the kite with Mister Max today. He was hopeless. He was making a real mess of it, and I didn't want him to crash it. So I took it off him in the end, and showed him how to do it. You should've seen me. It went so high. I mean, out of sight ... well, almost. You won't want to hear this, but I'm as good at flying kites as you ... well, almost. Anyway I'm a whole lot better at it than Mister Max, that's for sure. He's all right on the spool, I just have to nod and he lets out a little bit more. He's a bit slow. The last time I flew a kite with anyone else it was with you, Mahmoud. It was that day. Remember? Oh, Mahmoud, I don't want to remember, I don't want to, but I can't stop myself. It's my nightmare again, like a black hole waiting for me, and I'm falling. I'm falling into it. Mahmoud! Mahmoud! Help me!

I'm flying the kite, and I'm loving it. You're on the spool and you're going on and on about how Uncle Gasbag tries to keep us indoors, about how this is our hillside and no one can stop us flying our kites, not Uncle Yasser, not the soldiers, not the tanks, not anyone. I'm only half listening because I'm trying to concentrate on the kite. I'm doing well, too, diving it as fast as you, so fast I can

hear the rush and the roar of it in the wind
as it whizzes by over our heads. And I'm
laughing, laughing to see it up there, looping

and swooping. I'm still laughing when the roaring of the kite becomes a thunder and a throbbing in my ears. I'm so frightened because the ground underneath me is shaking and I can't understand why, until I see the helicopter coming up over the hilltop behind us and close, so close, almost touching the top of the kite tree. The sheep are going crazy, Mahmoud.

You're angry, Mahmoud. You're yelling at the helicopter, picking up a stone and throwing it, then another stone and another. The helicopter's right over us and we're being blown away by it, and I'm losing all control of the kite. It's spiralling crazily away down towards the road and it's crashing into the rocks. You're yelling at me to stay where I am, and then I see you racing down the hill after it. I've got my hands over my ears and I'm crying because I know already that something terrible is about to happen. I see the tank coming round the bend in the road before you do, and I'm screaming at you, Mahmoud, trying to warn you, but you can't hear me.

You're crouching over the kite now, and then you look up and see the tank. I know what you're going to do, and I know there's nothing I can do to stop you. You're too angry. "Mahmoud! Mahmoud! Don't do it!" But you do it. You run at the tank, shouting and

screaming at it, hurling stones at it. When they open fire you still don't stop. You only stop when you fall, and when you fall you're lying still, so still.

The soldiers tell me it's a mistake. They were firing warning shots, they say. They are sorry, they say. One of the soldiers is crying, but I'm not going to cry any more, not in front of them. There's blood. There's so much

blood. You are trying to tell me something. "Mend the kite, Said. Can you hear me? Mend the kite."

Yes, I can hear you. I'll mend the kite. Then I'll make another and another. I promise. I promise.

I'm still promising when the light goes out of your eyes, Mahmoud. You're looking at me and you're not seeing me.

• • •

But you are not dead, Mahmoud. I won't let you be dead. You will never be dead for me. I can hear your voice in my head. I know you're there when I talk to you. And you're in every one of the kites I make. When they fly, you fly. When you fly, you're alive.

You're flying high, looking down at me, waiting for the right wind, for the right moment to make the dream happen. I wish it would happen soon. I know it will, but I want it to be soon. I want Mister Max to see it with his own eyes. He doesn't believe it now, but he will then. He'll have to, won't he?

The girl in the blue headscarf believes it, I know that. Don't ask me how. I just know she does. She's there every day, sitting outside in her wheelchair watching me fly the kites. She's waiting for the moment. She's the girl you used to wave to. She wasn't in a wheelchair then, only afterwards. So it must be her, the girl who was injured in the ambush that day down on the road, the one whose mother was killed. She has binoculars. I can see the sunlight flashing on them sometimes. I'm sure she knows who I am, that I'm your little brother. If I know who she is, then why shouldn't she know who I am?

I think it must be her father who wheels

her out into the sun every day, checks the
brakes on the wheelchair and leaves her there.
Sometimes it must be her brother, who comes
with them, and who goes off to play football
with his friends. But she doesn't watch the
football. She watches me, and my kites, and
I watch her. We wave to each other, too,
whenever I send over a kite. In the last few
months she's been wheeling herself about more
and more, I think she's getting stronger each
day. We sit and look at one another over the
wall; me from under the kite tree, her from the
field below the settlement. There's something
strange happening between us, Mahmoud.
The more we look across at one another, the

more our thoughts seem to fly to each other over the wall. When I'm thinking of you, Mahmoud, I know she's thinking of you too. It's weird, I know, but I really can feel what she's thinking sometimes. And weirder still, I know she knows what I'm thinking too. She knows my dream. Sometimes I think maybe it was her dream before it was ever my dream. Perhaps we made it together. All I know for sure is that we dream the same dream. Don't ask me how.

Hey, Mahmoud, I want to tell Mister Max all about my dream and the girl in the wheelchair. I so wish I could speak again. I want to tell him all about you, Mahmoud, and the soldier who cried when he saw what he'd done. He would tell it truthfully to the world on the television, and then everyone would know what happened that day. Maybe if people really understood what bullets do then it would stop. He'll be going soon – tomorrow, he says, if his ankle's better. I hope it's not better. I want him to stay. I shall miss him when he's gone, him and his camera. But I'm making myself a promise, Mahmoud. I am deciding right now that when I grow up I shall make films like he does. I've worked it out. If I can't talk, then I'll tell our story in pictures, the story of you, Mahmoud, of our village, all about our kites and the wall and the settlement, and the girl in the blue headscarf who waves to us. I shall tell everyone about our nightmare and our dream, and about how one day we'll make it come true. It is my story, and the girl's story. Together we will make it come true.

Now I'm going to sleep. No more nightmares, only dreams. Goodnight, Mahmoud. Goodnight.

4th May

On a bus to visit
the settlement.
West Bank.
6.30 p.m.

After all that happened today, I have never wanted to meet anyone so much as that girl in the blue headscarf. So that's where I'm headed now, to talk to her, to find out her story. It's a bumpy old ride, but I have to try to write this down now whilst it's still fresh in my head. Think about it any longer, and I might persuade myself that none of it happened, that it was just a dream.

When I woke up this morning I could feel my ankle was a lot better, a lot stronger. There was still a weakness there, but most of the pain had gone. So I didn't need the crutch any more, just a stick. I said my goodbyes to the family after breakfast. I shall come back and see them again when the film's done and dusted. I want to show it to them. I want them to see I've been truthful, that I've told the story as it is, as it happened. The language has been a barrier, and I know my film will be the poorer for it. Without Uncle Yasser there to interpret, I felt awkward and inadequate sometimes. But I never once felt awkward with Said.

The whole family was there to see me off when I left the village this morning with Said and the sheep. As we went down the hill, Said's hand slipped into mine and I knew it wasn't

just to help me over the rocks. There was the same unspoken thought between us. We were friends, good friends. I didn't want to leave and he didn't want me to go. The sheep were in a clambering mood, their bleating and their bells noisy around us as we walked. We sat down together under the old olive tree. Said had brought the frame of his new kite with him, but he wasn't in the mood for working on it. He seemed lost in sadness. He was looking out over the valley, over the wall to the settlement beyond. A donkey brayed balefully from somewhere near by, winding itself up into a frenzy of misery. I decided it was better to get the parting over with quickly. I put my hand on his shoulder and let it rest there for a few moments. We were both too upset to say any other kind of goodbye. I got up, gathered up my rucksack and my equipment, and left him sitting there.

When I looked back a while later I saw that Said was busy with his kite. I decided to stop and film him, the perfect closing shot, just what I needed. I was just about organized and ready to film when Said sprang to his feet. The sheep were bounding away from him, scattering all over the hillside.

Then I saw the kites. The sky above the settlement was full of them, dozens of them, all colours and shapes, a kaleidoscope of kites. Like butterflies they danced and whirled around each other as they rose into the air. I could hear shrieks of joy, all coming from the other side of the wall. I saw the crowd of children gathered there, every one of them flying a kite. Some of the kites snagged each other and spiralled down to earth, but most sailed up magnificently, skywards. The settlers were running out of their houses to watch. Then, one after the other the kites were released and left to the wind, and on the wind they flew out over the wall towards us.

From behind us, from Said's village, the people came running too, as the kites began to land in amongst us and amongst the terrified sheep. Uncle Yasser picked one of them up. "You see what they wrote? *Shalom*," he said. "It says *shalom*. Can you believe that? And look, look!" On the other side of the kite they had drawn a dove. We soon discovered there was the same message, and the same drawing, on all of them.

Everywhere, on both sides of the wall, children were cheering and laughing and leaping up and down. I could see the girl in the wheelchair was struggling to stand up. When at last she made it, with the help of a couple of her friends, she took off her scarf and waved it wildly over her head.

All around me, Said's family, and many of the other villagers – mothers and fathers, grandmothers and grandfathers – began to clap, hesitantly at first. Soon everyone was joining in, Uncle Yasser too. But I noticed then that it was only the children who were whooping and whistling and laughing. The hillsides rang with their jubilation, with their exultation. It seemed to me like a glorious symphony of hope.

I had to be with Said at his moment of triumph. I stumbled as fast as I could back towards him, and as I came closer I could hear him laughing and shouting out loud, along with all the other children. I realized then, idiot that I was, that I had quite forgotten to film this miracle. But almost simultaneously I understood that it didn't matter anyway, that it was the laughter that mattered. It was laughter that would one day resonate so loud that this wall, like all the others, would come tumbling down. No trumpets needed, as they had been once at Jericho, only the laughter of children.

And then Said was running up to me, and taking me by the hands. "Mister Max, are you seeing it? The girl, she is sending back the kites. I knew she would do it. I knew it. It's her dream, it's my dream, it's our dream. But it's not a dream any more, is it? It's a real happening, isn't it? Are you hearing me, Mister Max? It's me, me speaking my voice, isn't it?" He put his head back, closed his eyes and shouted out loud to the sky above. "Hey, Mahmoud! Mahmoud! Can you hear me? Can you see this? The kites are flying, Mahmoud! The kites are flying!"

Afterword by Jeremy Bowen

Palestinian children like Said and Mahmoud really do fly kites. On hot afternoons in the West Bank a perfect kite-flying breeze blows out of the desert into the hills. In Gaza it comes in off the sea. Just like Said and Mahmoud, the children make their own kites – out of newspapers, old plastic bags and bits of wood. They turn what sounds like a pile of rubbish into something beautiful.

For the best part of a century Arabs and Jews have been fighting over this small piece of land that lies between the River Jordan and the Mediterranean Sea. The conflict often sends shockwaves around the world.

Many children have been wounded and killed. The pain that families on both sides feel when it happens is just the same. In my work as a reporter I have been to many funerals, and to homes full of sadness, where there are children who have seen brothers, sisters or parents killed.

My job is to help people understand why the conflict exists and why it doesn't stop. Sometimes that means trying to show what it is like to be a person caught up in it, at the very worst time of their lives. And sometimes, though not often enough, we find a few signs of hope, too.

Michael Morpurgo was 2003–2005 Children's Laureate, has written over one hundred books and is the winner of numerous awards, including the Whitbread Children's Book Award, the Blue Peter Book Award, the Smarties Book Prize and the Red House Children's Book Award. His books are translated and read around the world and his hugely popular novel *War Horse*, already a critically acclaimed stage play, is now also a blockbuster film. Michael and his wife, Clare, founded the charity Farms for City Children and live in Devon.

Laura Carlin is a graduate of the Royal College of Art and her work has featured in *Vogue*, the *Guardian* and *The New York Times*. Her children's book illustrations have won several awards, including the V&A Book Illustration Award and an honourable mention in the Bologna Ragazzi Award fiction category for *The Iron Man* by Ted Hughes. In 2015 she was awarded the Grand Prix at the prestigious Biennial of Illustrations Bratislava Awards and her most recent picture book, *The Promise* by Nicola Davies, was longlisted for the Kate Greenaway Medal. Laura lives in London.